All-Better
Bears

A Red Fox Book

Published by Random House Children's Books
20 Vauxhall Bridge Road, London SW1V 2SA

A division of The Random House Group Ltd
London Melbourne Sydney Auckland
Johannesburg and agencies throughout the world

Text copyright © Hiawyn Oram 1999
Illustrations copyright © Frédéric Joos 1999

1 3 5 7 9 10 8 6 4 2

First published in Great Britain by Andersen Press Ltd 1999
Red Fox edition 2000

Printed in Hong Kong by Midas Printing Ltd

THE RANDOM HOUSE GROUP Limited Reg. No. 954009
www.randomhouse.co.uk

ISBN 0 09 940118 5

All-Better Bears

Hiawyn Oram
illustrated by
Frédéric Joos

RED FOX

Baby Bear was playing on the floor . . .

and hit her head on the table.

"Never mind," said Big Bear. "I'll kiss it better."

Baby Bear was standing on a stool,
reaching for the highest shelf . . .

and slipped and bumped herself badly.

"Never mind," said Big Bear. "I'll kiss it better."

Baby Bear was playing in the playground.

Her best friend didn't want to be
her best friend anymore . . .

and her second best friend definitely didn't want
to be her second best friend anymore.

"Not a good day," sighed Baby Bear that night.

"Never mind," said Big Bear. "I'll kiss it better."

And the next day things did seem better.
Baby Bear made a new best friend . . .

and made her old best friend
her new second best friend.

But when she went home to tell Big Bear,
Big Bear was slumped on the sofa reading a letter.

"Is it bad news?" whispered Baby Bear.
"Very bad," sighed Big Bear.
"What? All over bad?" said Baby Bear.
"All over," said Big Bear.

"Never mind," said Baby Bear. "I'll kiss it better."
So Baby Bear kissed Big Bear's tum and Big Bear's
nose . . .

and Big Bear from Big Bear's top . . .

to Big Bear's toes . . .

and Big Bear
where it tickled . . .

and Big Bear where it didn't . . .

and Big Bear all over, all over and over
until Big Bear beamed and Big Bear laughed
and Big Bear cried, "Stop, Baby Bear, stop!
Though the bad news still isn't good,
it doesn't seem half so bad!"

"That's only because I forgot something!" cried Baby
Bear jumping up and running out of the room . . .

"...THE PLASTERS!"

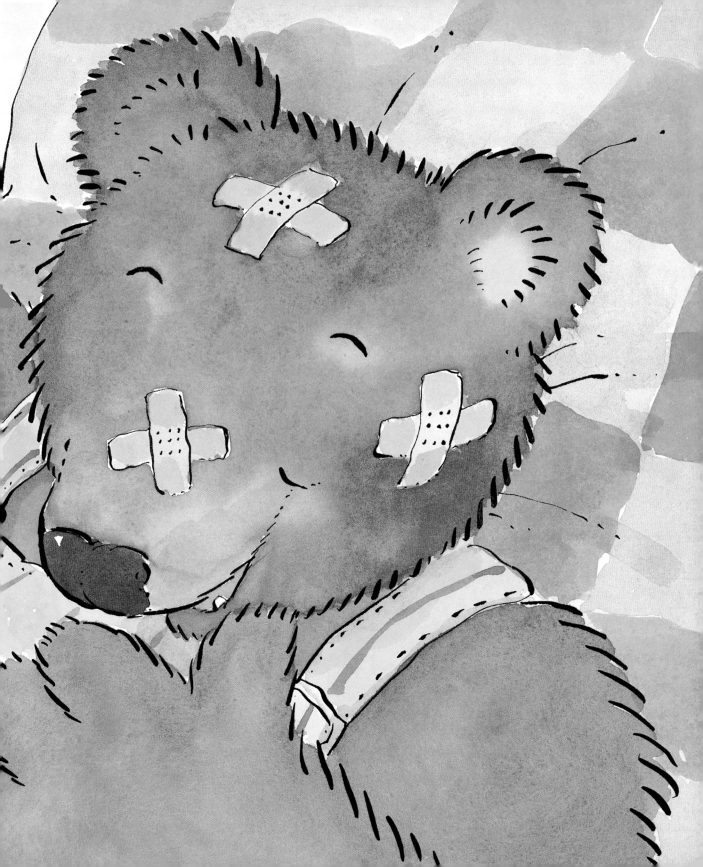

Some
bestselling Red Fox
picture books